PRAISE FOR
WICKED NIX

A JUNIOR LIBRARY GUILD SELECTION

★ "[Coakley] strikes a thoughtful balance between fairy tales and the realistic feelings of loss and love." —*Booklist*, starred review

"A spooky, compelling read."
—*Kirkus Reviews*

"Sheer delight." —Kathy Stinson, author of *Red Is Best* and *The Man with the Violin*

BY LENA COAKLEY

ILLUSTRATED BY
JAIME ZOLLARS

Harper_Trophy_

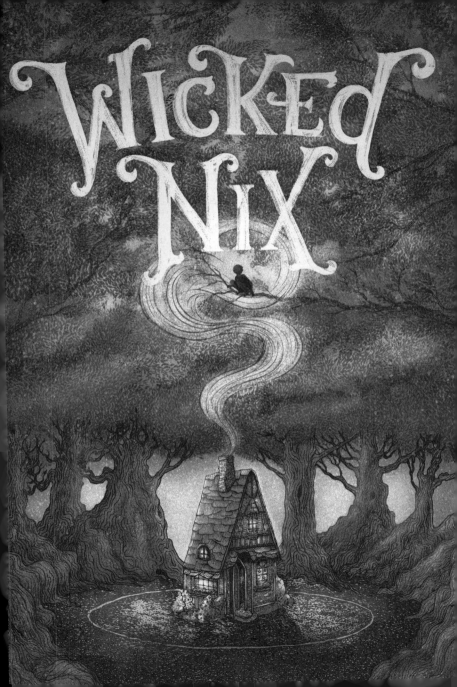

Wicked Nix
Text copyright © 2018 by Lena Coakley.
Illustrations copyright © 2018 by Jaime Zollars.
All rights reserved.

Published by Harper*Trophy* Canada™,
an imprint of HarperCollins Publishers Ltd

First published by HarperCollins Publishers Ltd
in a hardcover edition: 2018
This Harper*Trophy* Canada™ trade paperback edition: 2019

HarperCollins books may be purchased for educational,
business, or sales promotional use through our
Special Markets Department.

HarperCollins Publishers Ltd
Bay Adelaide Centre, East Tower
22 Adelaide Street West, 41st Floor
Toronto, Ontario, Canada
M5H 4E3

www.harpercollins.ca

Book design by Alyssa Nassner

Library and Archives Canada Cataloguing in Publication
information is available upon request.

ISBN 978-1-4434-5470-4

Printed and bound in the United States
LSC/H 9 8 7 6 5 4 3 2

For Jasmine

1

THERE IS SOMEONE IN THE FOREST.

Knock.

Knock. Knock.

It isn't the sound of one branch hitting another in the wind. It isn't the sound of a tree-pecker. It is the sound of someone who doesn't belong.

I climb higher in the old oak until I can see over the tops of the trees. I look in one direction all the way to Grandfather Mountain. I look in the other direction all the way to the village where the peoples live. Nothing seems wrong. Below me, the green forest sways in the wind. The crooked road winds through it like a scar.

I scan the road, up and down. I hate the idea of a people on it, but that is allowed as long as they keep moving. No. There is no one.

Knock.

Knock. Knock.

There! Over by the abandoned cottage. I see him! A little people the size of an ant. He's not on the road where he is allowed. He is in the forest.

There is a people in our forest.

* * *

I don't take the road. That's for them, and besides, my way is faster. I run along the deer path, leaping barefoot over roots and rocks. The screaming-blues dive at me, protecting their nest, but I am past their tree in a moment.

I stop short, almost falling. A spider-web stretches across the path, sparkling with dew. I go around, careful not to break the spider's pretty work, and I start to run again.

When I get near the cottage, I slow down. The knocking has stopped. I don't see anyone, but I know he's there. I can smell him, or at least I think I can. Like all peoples, he smells like soap and taking baths and eating with a fork. Horrible.

The door is wide open, and an old white cow stands in the garden patch, chewing weeds.

In front of the cottage is the kind of tree whose leaves look shivery when the wind blows. It is called a shivery tree. I climb it and hide in the branches. Even with my bent arm, no one in the forest climbs as well as I do.

A people comes out. A man-people. He is tallish and oldish and baldish.

I see that he has some big nails in one hand and a hammer in the other. I shrink back, afraid. A nail would burn me. Anything made of iron would burn me.

The man-people climbs a ladder and bangs the nails into the roof: *knock, knock, knock*. He's fixing the house. He thinks he can live here. In our forest.

"Badness!" I cry. "This forest belongs to the fairies. You cannot stay."

The man-people is so surprised he nearly falls off the ladder.

"Who's there?" he says, scanning the trees. "Let me see you."

I laugh my wickedest laugh. "You don't want that. A people like you would scream and run away if you saw my face, and your hair would turn white as bone forever, for I am Wicked Nix, the foulest of the fairies."

"Oh," he says.

"Leave at once!"

"But . . ." The man-people climbs down the ladder and squints up into the shivery tree. "But it's my home, you know."

This makes me angry. I make my voice low, like the growl of a bear. "I warn you. If you don't leave, I will put a curse upon your garden so that nothing grows but thorns. I will put a spell upon your hearth so that your fire always smokes. I will turn your well water into skunk spit and . . . and frog pee. I will give your cow wings, and she will fly to the moon!"

I can see he is afraid now. I am sure he is about to beg my fairy pardon. I am sure he is about to leave and never come back. I am very surprised when he says:

"Do your worst, Wicked Nix, foulest of the fairies! This cottage is mine, and I will never leave!"

2

I SPEND THE NIGHT THROWING rocks and sticks and pinecones at the man-people's roof, but he just stays inside.

The truth is, I don't know how to put a curse on his garden so that nothing grows but thorns. I don't know how to put a spell on his hearth or his well water. And I certainly don't know how to give a cow wings.

Why did the Good Queen have to leave and put me in charge of the forest? I wonder. So many of her other fairies have more magic than me.

I go back to my nest in the old oak tree, feeling grouchy as a badger. Usually my nest is very comfortable—it's made from blankets and ropes and other things I took from the village when no one was looking—but today I toss and turn in my hammock among the branches.

When I finally fall asleep, I dream of the Summer Country. That's where all the fairies are now—all the fairies but me. Time passes slow and sweet as honey there, and no one is ever cold or hungry. In my dream, I can see the Summer Country just ahead. All my fairy friends are waving at me—Fleet and Flit and Wing and Dart. I run and run, but I can't seem to get there.

The sun is high when I wake up. I have slept the morning away. Above me, in the pattern of green leaves, there is a face. It shifts and swishes in the breeze.

"Oh, Mr. Green," I say. "I'm in trouble."

I don't know who Mr. Green is, exactly, but whenever I need him, he is there—sometimes in the ripples on the river, sometimes in the sunlight on the forest floor. He gives me good advice.

"What is it?" His voice is whispery, like leaves rustling.

"My stomach. It feels like the time I ate rocks."

"Hmm. Hungry then."

"No!"

I sit up. Now I see Mr. Green's face in the wrinkly bark of my oak tree. His eyes are knots, and his nose is a little branch.

"It's that man-people! He's in the abandoned cottage where he's not allowed. What if the Good Queen of the Fairies comes back and finds him living here?"

"Peoples live in cottages. It's what they do."

"That's no help. How can I get rid of him?"

"Hmmm. Let me think. Let me think."

I try to be patient, but Mr. Green thinks for a long time. A fuzzy caterpillar inches along one of the ropes of my nest. I pick it up carefully and put it on a leaf, which it starts to chew. My stomach gives a gigantic rumble.

"I knew it," says Mr. Green. "Breakfast is what you need. Breakfast solves most of your problems, Nix."

"A fairy only needs an acorn for breakfast." My stomach rumbles again. "Or maybe two."

I stand up on a branch, holding the trunk of the old oak tree, and look down over the forest. I see no sign of the people, but I know he's there.

"Please help me," I say. "How can I make him leave when I have no magic?"

Now Mr. Green's face is huge. His eyebrows are shaggy pine trees. His smile is the curve of the river, far away, but I still hear his voice at my ear.

"Village," he says. "Food and drink."

"A fairy only needs a dewdrop to drink," I say, "and a flower petal for a cup."

"A dewdrop," he says, chuckling. "A flower."

The whole forest shakes, and suddenly I am inside Mr. Green's laughter. It sounds like branches creaking.

"Fine!" I shout. "Don't help. I'll do it myself."

* * *

I do not take Mr. Green's advice and go to the village. Instead, I go to the cottage again.

A fairy doesn't need magic to make mischief, I tell myself. I will steal things. I will break things. I will cause ruin and disaster! And if none of that works, I will show that man-people my foul face, and he will run away in terror.

The cottage has changed since yesterday. The vines that covered it have all been pulled away. Foxes and squirrels and other forest animals are carved around the door.

Who used to live here? I wonder. *Who made this pretty place? Surely not the horrible man-people with the nails.*

The garden patch is a square of dirt now, ready for planting. All the weeds are piled high by the side of the cottage.

I remember what I told him: *I will curse your garden so that nothing grows but thorns.* That man-people will not see one green shoot in this new garden, I promise myself.

I want to get closer to see what else he's done, but just as I am about to take a step, I see it: a line of salt! Someone has made a big, white circle all around the cottage, the garden, and the little barn. This is powerful magic, meant to keep a fairy out. If I set one foot over that line, I will shrivel like a garden slug, down and down, until I am only the size of a bug.

I run back behind the shivery tree, my heart bumping in my chest.

Oh, I think. *That man-people. He is rotten. He is mean. But he knows things about fairies.*

My stomach rumbles and groans. I remember Mr. Green's advice.

Of course! He didn't want me to go to the village just for breakfast. He must want me to talk to Rose the Wise. She'll know what to do about my people problem.

"Why didn't you just say that in the first place, Mr. Green?" I say.

3

I TAKE THE DEER PATH TO THE forest's edge, where the village begins. The peoples here are afraid of fairies, as they should be. They know that if we are angry, we will make their chickens lay black eggs or their cows give sour milk, and so they leave gifts to make us happy.

On a big stone in someone's yard I see a lump of something tied in a handkerchief. Quick as an owl, I swoop in and take it away, back to the woods. It's a piece of cheese. I gobble half of it and save the rest for later.

At the back of another house is an old well where someone has left a bowl of milk. There are some flies in it, but I don't mind a few flies.

I go from house to house finding my gifts.

The peoples have pleased me today. I'm glad I do not have to punish them. The truth is, it's hard to convince a chicken to lay black eggs—and most of the time when I tell a cow to give sour milk, she just stares at me as if she doesn't understand what I'm saying.

I go to the littlest house with the prettiest garden, where I usually find the best gift of all. Today I find someone about to eat it.

Rose the Wise is a little girl-people, but not an ordinary little girl-people. She has many strange and amazing powers.

I spy on her as she sits at a tree-stump table at the end of her garden. Her hair is tied with ribbons into two fuzzy puffs. She is singing a song to herself. On the stump is a white plate with a lovely piece of honeycomb on it.

"Oh, Nix. Oh, Nix. Can I have some of that honeycomb?" she sings. "Yes, you may. Yes, you may."

I have noticed that Rose often sings songs or talks to me, even when she doesn't know I'm there. Or perhaps she always knows I'm there. Rose is a mysterious people, so it's hard to say.

She picks up my honeycomb and nibbles the edge. "Now can I have some more, more, more?" she sings.

"No, you may not. No, you may not," I sing as I jump out from behind a tree.

She laughs and laughs. This is how I know that in spite of being a people, Rose has powerful magic. Anyone else would scream and run away if they saw my face, and their hair would turn white as bone forever, for I am Wicked Nix, the foulest of the fairies.

Rose gets up and dances around and around in circles on the grass. "Nix is here. Nix is here."

I am in a hurry to get back to the abandoned cottage, but I know that there is no rushing Rose when she is dancing around. I quickly eat the honeycomb.

Finally, she plops down heavily at our tree-stump table. Her face turns sad. "Poor arm," she says, pointing. Rose has a tender heart and says this every time I come.

I lick my sticky fingers. "The queen will fix it. When she comes back."

Last year, when I was left behind by the other fairies, I didn't know how to live in the forest. At first I slept on the ground, but it got colder and colder. The wolves came down from Grandfather Mountain, sniffing for food. One morning I woke up and a wolf was sniffing *me*. He went away, but I knew that the next day or the day after that, he would be hungry enough to try and eat me.

It was Mr. Green who told me to make a nest in the trees using blankets and laundry ropes from the village, but it takes practice to sleep in a nest. I fell out and my arm got bent, but it doesn't hurt anymore.

"Let's have some tea," I say.

One of Rose's strange and amazing powers is that she can conjure invisible tea out of thin air.

"Hold out your cup," she says.

I hold out my hand, watching Rose. She doesn't make any magical sign. She doesn't even say any magic words. She just takes hold of an invisible teapot and pours the invisible tea into the invisible cup that has appeared in my hand.

I get shivers up and down my arms, feeling her great power all around me.

"What kind is it?" I whisper.

"It's berries tea," she says. "Here is the sugar."

She puts down the invisible teapot and spoons the invisible sugar into my cup.

I cannot feel the cup, but I know it's there. Carefully, I blow on the tea.

"Is it blackberries?"

"Blackberries and redberries and all the berries," she says.

I take a sip. Invisible tea is hard to taste. You have to concentrate.

"Delicious," I say.

Rose smiles. She is as beautiful as the Good Queen herself when she smiles— and thinking of the Good Queen makes me remember why I'm here.

"Rose, I have a problem. There is a people in the forest."

Her eyes widen. She sets down her invisible teacup. Rose knows the rules— and she understands when something is serious. "On the road?"

I shake my head slowly. "No. He is not on the road."

She puts her hand over her mouth. "Oh dear, oh dear. What will you do?"

My stomach feels tight all of a sudden. "I don't know."

I look around the garden. When the flowers are at their prettiest, that's when the Good Queen comes back— and Rose's garden is so very pretty. The twinkly stars are all in bloom, with rows of purple puff-puffs behind them. Bees buzz around the butter yellows. It must be very close to Midsummer's Eve, the night when the fairies come to the forest to dance. What if the man-people hasn't left by then? Will the queen be angry? Will she let me come home?

"Can you help me, Rose?" I ask.

She thinks for a moment. "Fairies play tricks—so you must play a trick on that man. A very tricky trick."

"I wish I could, but he has put a ring of salt around his cottage! If I go near, I will shrivel like a garden slug, down and down, until I am the size of a bug."

"Oh, Nix! Oh, Nix!" Rose sings at me. She gets up and twirls around.

I can't complain. She's been sitting a long time for her.

"You must sing this magic song," she sings. "Ha-ha, ma-ta, fa-fa-la. Then you will not get small."

"Ha-ha, ma-fa, fa-la-la?"

Rose stops her dancing. "Nooo," she says. "Don't sing that. That will make you shrivel, down and down, until you disappear."

"Oh."

She twirls again. "Ha-ha, ma-ta, fa-fa-la."

"Ha-ha, ma-ta, fa-fa-la," I say.

"Now dance with me!"

I get up and dance with Rose, around and around, repeating the magic words again and again until I know them by heart.

4

ROSE THE WISE SAYS THAT I MUST
play a trick on the horrible man-people.
A tricky trick. Ideas wriggle in my mind.
That man-people thinks he is safe behind
his ring of salt, but I know better.

I wait until it's dark and the moon rises.
Then I set out. I bring a basket that a vil-
lager gave me as a gift—or maybe he just

left it in his yard. It's not stealing if you're a fairy.

The air is warm, and the nighty-night bugs are very loud. I go through the fairy meadow. It is bright with moonlight and stars. A breeze rustles the grass, and I see Mr. Green's face.

"Soon, soon, soon," he whispers. I smile and wave as I go by.

Soon they will come—that's what he means. Soon fairy feet will trample this grass with their dancing. The meadow is waiting for them, just as I am, waiting for Midsummer's Eve.

I climb a small hill in the middle of the meadow. This is where my fairy friends disappeared a year ago. One moment the hill was covered with tents and torches and laughter. All the fairies were dancing— some with antlers on their heads or animal faces, some with wings like moths or dragonflies. I was dancing, too. In the center was the Good Queen in her cloak of midnight.

The next thing I knew, everyone was gone.

I have danced in the fairy meadow on Midsummer's Eve many times, and afterward I always went back with the others to the Summer Country, where time passes slow and sweet as honey and everything is like a dream. I never thought about how I got there. I never asked.

During the past year, I have returned to this meadow many times. I look for a secret door in the hill, but I never find one; I look for the hidden path to lead me home, but I never see it. It must have been magic that made everyone disappear, the Good Queen's magic.

I'm sure she did not forget me, though. I'm sure she loves me. She once pulled a star down from the sky for me—that's how I know. She must have left me here to protect the forest. She must have left me here because she trusts me more than all of the others.

I leave the meadow and go along the windy path. I cross the river on slippery stones. Finally, I get to the bramble patch where the don't-eat-me berries grow. Careful not to prick myself, I break off some thorny sticks, putting them in my basket.

After that I find the quiet place in the forest, where the green moss grows thick under my feet. Here I stop and fill my basket with big clumps, putting them on top of the sticks.

The moss is soft, and the dirt smells good. All of a sudden, an old memory of the Good Queen comes to me.

Once, I leaned into her body, my cheek on her thigh, and her dress against my face was as soft as this moss.

"I miss you," I say out loud.

I put some moss against my cheek. I close my eyes. A breeze comes, and it feels just like her fingers touching my hair.

"I will protect the forest for you," I say. "When you come back, you will be proud of me."

Even before I see the man-people's cottage, I can feel the bad magic of the line of salt. It makes my basket heavier. It makes the night colder. It makes all the spit go out of my mouth. Can I still sing the song if I don't have any spit? I don't want to shrivel down and down to the size of a bug.

"Ha-ha, ma-ta, fa-fa-la," I try to sing. My voice sounds like a whisper.

Slowly, slowly, I put one foot over the line of salt.

"Ha-ha, ma-ta, fa-fa-la. Ha-ha, ma-ta, fa-fa-la."

I move my weight to the front foot. "Ha-ha, ma-ta, fa-fa-la." I put my other foot over the line.

I'm across!

I put down my basket and look at my body in the moonlight. I'm still here. And I'm not bug-size. I want to dance and spin like Rose would, but I have work to do.

I told the man-people I would curse his hearth so that his fire always smoked, and so I climb his ladder and stuff his chimney with the green moss. While I'm there, I pull off all of the new shingles—careful not to touch the nails—and I toss them down onto the grass.

I told the man-people that I would curse his garden so that it grew only thorns, and so I take my thorny sticks and plant them deep into the dirt of his garden, sticking them up as if they'd grown there.

Then I climb into the shivery tree and wait. By this time there is a pink glow behind Grandfather Mountain. It is almost morning, and I want to be there when the man-people sees all my mischief.

I doze off while watching the cottage, but when I hear the man-people's cries, I wake with a start. The shutters fly open, and smoke pours out. He must have tried to light his fire. A moment later, he runs outside.

"Oh, no! Oh, no!" he says. How funny he looks in his bare feet and nightshirt with his sleeping cap on.

I giggle into my hand. Then my giggling turns to laughter.

"I hear you, fairy!" the man-people says.

"Yes, it is me!" I shout. "I have magic against your line of salt. Now leave and never come back!"

The man-people glares up into the tree. "I don't need a fire. I will eat my food raw."

"Food? What food?" I say, laughing again. I shake a branch, making all the leaves rustle. "Where will you grow it?"

Then the man-people runs to his garden. He touches one of the thorny sticks, then jumps back with a cry, putting his finger in his mouth.

"Leave or starve, badness!" I shout.

His face is bright pink. *Will he faint?* I wonder. Will he get down on his knees and beg me to remove my curse?

"This is my home," the evil man-people yells, "and I will never leave, Wicked Nix!"

Then he goes back into his cottage and slams the door.

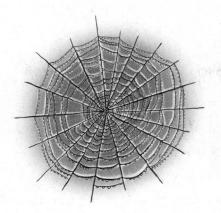

5

I WAIT AND WAIT IN THE SHIVERY
tree. I can't believe what the man-people
said. I'm sure he is packing up his things.
In a moment, he will come out of the door,
get his cow, and travel back down the road
to wherever it is he came from.

He doesn't come out.

All the birds are awake now, singing their good-morning songs, and I haven't even been to sleep yet. I go back to my nest in the old oak.

"Check your knots," says Mr. Green. His face is high above me in a rain cloud.

I sigh and tighten all the knots in all my ropes and blankets. If they get loose, I might fall out of the oak tree again.

"Put the sheet on top. It's going to rain."

"Do you tell all the birds and squirrels how to build *their* nests?" I snap.

"As a matter of fact, I do," Mr. Green says.

"Oh." I think of all the birds and squirrels in the forest and decide Mr. Green must be very busy. "Well. All right then."

I make a roof for my nest, then I lie down and pull a blanket over me. I'm about to close my eyes, when I have an idea.

"Mr. Green, you could get rid of that man-people for me."

"Hmmm. I don't know." His face is teeny-tiny, hiding in the splotches of blue-green fungus on a branch. "He hasn't done anything wrong."

"Wrong! He's a people living in the fairy forest. It's not allowed."

"Those aren't *my* rules."

I turn my back to him. "Well, I don't need you, anyway. I just have to change that man-people's well water into skunk spit and frog pee. It's just—I don't know how I'll do it."

"Nix!" says Mr. Green, and the whole tree quivers with his voice. I pull the blanket over my head. "You're not going to hurt any of my frogs or my skunks, are you?"

"Mr. Green!" My voice is muffled in the blanket. "You know I would never do that."

"Humph. Yes. I suppose I do."

For a while he says nothing, only sighs and whistles with the wind as the storm gathers. The air smells like rain. My nest sways back and forth. I know I should sleep, but I'm worried.

"Why do you really want to get rid of him?" Mr. Green asks.

"You know," I say. "For the queen. She'll be angry to find a people in the forest."

"And what will she do if she's angry?"

The question sits in my chest like something heavy. The queen can do many terrible things—turn a fairy into a toad, freeze rivers with her icy breath, make lightning fall from the sky—but that's not what I'm afraid of. I answer so softly I can hardly hear myself over the sound of the wind. "She might leave me again."

"Nix," Mr. Green says, and with that the rain begins to fall.

I lift the blanket a little and see Mr. Green's face in the shifting raindrops.

"I don't know what I did wrong," I tell him, "but I must have done something. I don't think I could spend another year in the forest, even with your help. I get so cold, and I get so hungry. If she leaves me again, I think . . . I think I'll die, Mr. Green."

I pull the blanket over my head again and squeeze my eyes tight.

"Listen to the rain," Mr. Green says softly, "and perhaps the answers you are looking for will come to you while you sleep."

I yawn. Mr. Green always give good advice, and so I do what he says and listen to the rain go *pittery, pattery, pittery, pattery*.

The roof I made isn't very good, but somehow I stay dry. Maybe Mr. Green catches all the raindrops with his leafy fingers.

Pittery, pattery, pittery, pattery, pittery, pattery.

Mr. Green is right: The answer *does* come to me in the sound of the rain. When I wake up, I've thought of a new trick.

The forest smells fresh and clean as I run along the deer path. The sun glitters on wet leaves. Even though I won't play my trick until tonight, I need to know what the man-people has done while I was sleeping.

I am right. He *has* done things. The cottage is different again. More grass and weeds have been pulled up, and now I can see a path of white stones leading to the door.

Something hangs in the open window. A lot of somethings. When I get closer, I see carved wooden birds and animals, swinging on strings.

Leave the cottage alone! I want to yell. *Stop changing it!*

I get the strangest feeling deep in my fairy bones. Even if peoples didn't make the queen angry, I would still want to get this man-people out. It is wrong for him to be here. Very wrong. He is disturbing something that should stay asleep. The abandoned cottage must stay as it always has been: empty and forgotten.

I am about to leave, but then I notice something. The line of salt has washed away, but now nails and thimbles and other bits of iron are hiding in the wet grass. I almost missed them! This is terrible magic against fairies. Any one of those iron things could burn a hole right through my foot if I stepped on it.

I notice something else. Hanging on the door and over the windows are chains of daisies. Fairies love most flowers, but daisies are evil. They put fairies into a deep sleep. If I go near one, I will fall down snoring in the grass, and then I will be at the man-people's mercy.

How will I get near enough to play my trick? I wonder.

I turn and run into the forest. Rose the Wise will know the answer.

6

THE FLOWERS IN ROSE'S GARDEN
are all drooping from the rain, and Rose is
drooping, too. She is sitting on the stump,
her back to the house. Her face is shiny
with tears.

"What's the matter?" I ask.

Her words come out in gulps. "My
mother says I can't sit still."

"You can't."

Rose lets out a wail.

"I'm sorry!" I say. "I didn't mean it. I'm sure you can."

She falls to the ground and sobs into the wet earth. "No. It's true. I can't."

I lie down, my face right next to hers. "Why would anybody want to sit still, anyway?"

She looks into my eyes. "To eat a nice dinner at the table. To have my hair brushed."

I shudder. People-y things. "I've never had my hair brushed, and I never will."

She touches my hair. "It's got sticks in it."

I sit up and say proudly, "That's right. And probably bugs, too."

Rose also sits up and wipes her face with the sleeve of her dress. "I'm going to live in the forest with you. I'm going to put sticks in my hair and be a fairy."

I start to remind her that you can't just *decide* to be a fairy, but Rose has already gotten up and is gathering sticks from the ground. I don't want her to cry again.

"Sometimes," I tell her, "the Good Queen of the Fairies will let a people come live with her in the Summer Country. I never saw one there, but I heard it's true. It has to be a very special people, though."

Rose pushes sticks under the ribbons in her hair. "What's the Summer Country?"

I'm surprised she doesn't know about it. "It's the fairy kingdom under the hill. Time passes slow and sweet as honey there, and everything is like a dream."

"Do you have to sit still there?"

"You don't have to do anything you don't want to."

"Oh," Rose says with a twirl. "I want to come!"

"Maybe you could," I say. "All my friends are there—Fleet and Flit and Wing and Dart. They're fairies, like me. In the Summer Country, everyone laughs and tells stories all day, and we listen to the queen's songs, which are the most beautiful songs in the world, and we eat fruit from the silver trees, which is the most delicious food in the world, and no one is ever cold or lonely or unhappy."

Rose climbs up on the stump, opens her arms, and sings as if to an audience, "I'm going to beeeee ... a little faireeeee ... in the Summer Countreeee!"

"Not a fairy, a guest," I say. "And the queen will have to like you."

"She will like meeeeee! Because I am meeeeee!"

I think this is probably true. Rose is so wise, and she doesn't scream and run away when she sees my face. Surely the queen would see that she's not like most peoples.

"I suppose I could ask her on Midsummer's Eve. But Rose, that man-people is still in the forest. Rose, please stop singing for a minute . . ."

"I will never eat peeeeeeeeas! I will never say pleeeeeeeeeease! I won't clean my rooooooom! I won't use a brooooooom! When I'm a faireeeeee! In the Summer Countreeeee! How happy I'll beeeeeee!"

"Rose, the queen will be in a very bad mood if that man-people is still in the forest when she gets here. She won't be interested in hearing about any other peoples then—even special ones like you."

"You must play a triiiiiiick!"

"Yes, I know, but the man-people has put daisy chains on his door. That's powerful magic. I don't know what to do."

"Take this magic stiiiiiiiiick!"

Rose takes a stick from her hair and gives it to me. It looks like any ordinary stick, but when I hold it in my hand, I can feel its magic. I put it carefully behind my ear.

"Thank you!" I say. "But he's got nails and thimbles and other iron things in the grass, too. If I step on one, it will burn a hole right through my poor fairy foot!"

"Here's what you must dooooo!" Rose sings, but before she can finish, another voice calls out.

"Ros-ie!"

Quickly, I hide behind a tree. A woman-people is standing on the steps of Rose's house, drying her hands on an apron. The apron is the same flowery material as Rose's dress.

"What is that terrible noise you're making? What are you doing out there?"

Rose turns around on her stump. "I'm singing to a fairy, Mummy!"

Rose's mother takes a few steps toward the garden, frowning at the forest. She looks and looks, but she doesn't see me.

"Fairies are nothing to pretend about," she finally says. "They're dangerous. Come inside."

"Yes, Mummy!"

She climbs down from the stump and runs toward the door, but a moment later she comes back. "Here's what you must

dooooooo!" she sings. "You must wear a shoooooooooooe! Or twoooooooo!"

"Rose!" her mother shouts, and Rose scampers to her. "That dress was clean a minute ago, and now there's mud all over it, and where is your hair ribbon?"

Poor Rose, I think, as she disappears through the door. I can't imagine someone so wise having to do the bidding of an ordinary people.

If I do get rid of that man-people, I think, and if the queen is in a good mood on Midsummer's Eve, I will ask if Rose can come and live with us. Then she will never have to sit still or brush her hair or eat peas ever again.

7

IT'S DARK. GRANDMOTHER MOON IS round and fat. I go a different way tonight, through the valley where the thin-white-lady trees grow with their papery bark. These are my favorite trees, but I never say this out loud in case other trees are listening.

I startle a fox, who stares at me with glowing yellow eyes. I nod a greeting, and he runs away, going about his business.

Finally, I get to the pond where the stinkflowers grow. I wade in, mud squishing between my toes. All around me, moon-bugs go on and off, on and off, their light reflected in the water. I find the smelliest stinkflowers and put them into my basket.

When I am near the man-people's house, I gather some leaves and vines, tying them around my feet. Rose said I must "wear a shoe," but fairies never wear shoes. I think this is what she meant. If I protect my feet, the iron things in the grass cannot hurt me. I inch toward the cottage, touching the stick behind my ear, hoping it is powerful enough to keep away the sleepy magic of the daisy chains.

I am thinking so much about shoes and sticks and daisies and iron that I almost don't notice the ring of salt! He must have made a new one after the first washed away in the rain. Evil man-people. He is using all the tricks he knows against me tonight.

"Ha-ha, ma-ta, fa-fa-la," I whisper. I cross the white line, but I do not shrink.

Slowly, I go toward the house. I accidentally step on a horseshoe, but I am not burned.

I yawn, and for a moment I think the spell of the daisy chains must be working, but I poke myself in the arm with the magic stick, and I don't feel tired at all.

"Thank you, Rose," I whisper.

I take my basket to the well at the side of the house. I told the man-people I would turn his well water into skunk spit and frog pee, and so—holding my breath—I dump in the stinkflowers. I don't know exactly what skunk spit and frog pee smells like, but I think this will be just as bad.

I am about to go back over the line of salt when I see that the man-people has left one of his windows open. The carved wooden animals spin on their strings. I come closer, wondering what kind of animals they are.

I can feel the magic of the daisy chains trying to make me yawn. My mouth opens wide. The more I think about not yawning, the more I want to. I poke myself with the stick a few more times.

I touch one of the animals. It has a tail like a fish and two long tusks coming from its mouth. I've never seen anything like it in the forest.

I give it a tug, then another. It's not stealing if you're a fairy.

Ping. The string snaps. It's only a little noise, but from inside the house, a voice calls, "Who's there?"

I run toward the cover of the bushes. I can't see the line of salt, but I sing "Ha-ha, ma-ta, fa-fa-la" again and again under my breath.

The man-people comes out of the house, holding a lantern. From the bushes I can see his face change as he smells the stinkflowers.

"Oh, no!" he cries, running to the side of the house.

I laugh as he puts his whole head down the well. Then he pulls it back with a groan, his hand over his nose. "Skunk spit and frog pee! Oh, horrible fairies!"

Yes, we fairies are *horrible,* I think, *and I am the horriblest of them all!*

What will he do now? I wonder, peeking through the branches of my bush. I hope he bursts into tears. I hope he runs off down the road and never returns. But the man-people only stands for a long time. His shoulders slump. Then, slowly, he walks toward his door.

"Ouch!" he says, jumping on one foot. He has stepped on one of his own nails in the grass. This should be funny, too, but for some reason I don't laugh.

The man-people sits down in the dirt, the lantern beside him, and puts his face in his hands. A moment ago I wanted him to burst into tears, but now he's really crying—and it makes my stomach feel like the time I ate too many green apples.

He pulls off his nightcap and uses it to wipe his eyes. "I don't need a well, Nix, foulest of the fairies. I'll get my water from the river."

Can it be? I think. *I made him cry, and he is still not going to leave?*

The man-people stands up again.

"Listen to me, Wicked Nix, and listen well! I have a magic powder that can turn a fairy invisible, like a ghost. One touch of it, and no one will see you, no one will hear you—not your fairy friends, not even the queen herself. You will reach out to them, and your hand will pass right through. They won't feel you. They won't know you're there, though you will cry and call and beg."

The words put an icy chill in my heart. Not to be seen or heard or felt, not even by the queen—it would be too awful.

"I made this powder out of dried troll blood and witches' tears and ground-up fairy wings," the man-people says. "And I am going to sprinkle it all over this place."

I am shaking in the bushes now. How did he get ground-up fairy wings? I feel faint just thinking about it.

"Why do you hate us so much?" I shout.

The man-people raises his lantern, looking for me. "I have my reasons. Why do you want me to leave so badly?"

"I would do anything for my queen."

The man-people picks up a long stick and moves toward me. "I know all about *her*. She is cold and cruel."

I should not let him know where I am, but I cannot help but answer. "Liar!" I shout. "The queen is kind and wonderful. She loves me."

"Fairies are never kind," he says, jabbing his stick into the leaves beside me. "And they cannot love."

I run away so his poking stick cannot find me.

8

I CLIMB THE OLD OAK TREE IN THE dark, scrambling from branch to branch until I reach my nest. There is a hollow place in the trunk where I keep my treasures. I feel for it and put the strange carved animal inside.

I can't stop thinking about what the man-people said, that fairies are never kind and cannot love. I am kind, I think. And I love lots of things.

Then I remember all the tricks I have played—how proud I was to be so horrible, how I hoped the man-people would burst into tears. I remember that my friends Fleet and Flit and the others are always telling mean stories about the "stupid peoples" they have known.

I think about one of those stories now, the story of the singer with the fiery red hair. He was a man-people who came to watch the fairies dance one Midsummer's Eve. I don't remember him, but I heard the story many times in the Summer Country.

Usually a people who bothers the fairies during their dance is turned into a toad, but this man-people was different. Maybe it was his handsome face, or maybe it was his lovely singing voice, but for some reason the Good

Queen took a liking to him. She invited him to come with us to the Summer Country, where time flows slow and sweet as honey and everything is like a dream.

After a while, though, the singer with the fiery red hair grew to pining for the peoples he had left back home. He could only sing sad songs, which the queen didn't like, and his handsome face was always frowning. The queen grew tired of his moping and cast him out.

But when the singer returned to the people world, he found that everything had changed. He had only aged a few years, but the girl he had left behind was a white-haired old woman, and everyone else he knew was dead and gone.

The fairies always find this story very funny. They laugh and laugh when they tell it and say, "What a stupid people he was."

I used to say it, too, "what a stupid people," and then the fairies would laugh even louder.

Now, I lean up against the trunk of the old oak, wondering how I could have found such a story funny. *Are we fairies cruel?* I wonder. *Can we love?*

I put my hands in the hollow of the oak tree, feeling for my other treasures. I have a white stone I found by the river that looks like a face. I have a robin redbelly egg, blue as sky, that never became a bird. Best of all I have my star, a real star given to me by the Good Queen.

I find it and pull it out.

Some might think stars are made of fire, but I know they are made of wood and painted silver, with little bits of mirror in the points to make them shine.

I press my star tightly in my hand. The memory of getting it is old and faded, but it is as precious as the star itself. The Good Queen was singing, and I was looking up at her. With a touch of her hand, she made each star spin above our heads.

I wanted to touch one, too. I reached and reached. Finally, the Good Queen took pity on me and pulled a star from the sky. She put it in my hand, and I laughed and laughed as all the other stars whirled and bobbed and glittered.

Perhaps it's true that fairies can be cruel, but we can be kind, too—and I will always have my star to prove that once the Good Queen loved me.

9

THE NEXT MORNING, I GO STRAIGHT to the village. My gifts are particularly good, and no one has forgotten, but I notice that many houses have wreaths of daisies on their door, or horseshoes with their ends pointing up, or tied bunches of smelly sticks.

When I get to the littlest house with the prettiest garden, I find a whole jar of jam sitting on the stump. This is a good gift because of the jam and also because of the jar, which I can use to put things in—but for now, I leave it where it is.

Rose is not in the garden, and so I creep toward the house. I try not to think about the fact that it is all put together with iron nails. Usually I don't like to get so close to where peoples do their people-y things—like cooking with fire and eating on plates—but I need Rose's help today more than ever.

I peek through the window and see her standing at a big table with her mother. They are making bread, but I'm not sure how I know this because it's not something fairies ever do.

Rose's mother has a big lump of dough in front of her, and Rose has a little lump. The table is white with flour. Rose's mother is singing a song.

Daughter, oh daughter, my heart is wide.
All of your dreams can fit inside.
Swim the sea bottom or sail to a star,
My love is with you wherever you are.

The music of the song does strange things. It slips and slithers in and out of my ears and over my skin and down the back of my neck. It shakes loose old memories.

Did I make bread like this once? Did the Good Queen of the Fairies wear an apron covered with flour and sing to me? I know it can't be possible, but it seems so real.

Rose looks up from her dough and sees me at the window. Quickly, I duck my head.

"I'm going out, Mummy!" I hear her shout.

"Wait, wait," her mother tells her.

I run to the end of the garden, where I can hide in the bushes. A few minutes later, Rose comes. She smiles when she sees me, but I shrink back.

"Ugh!" I say, pointing at the daisy chain around her neck. "What's that?"

"Mummy made it. So the fairies don't steal me."

"It will make me fall into a deep sleep!"

She shakes her head, pointing. "You still have the stick."

I find the stick behind my ear and poke myself a few times. "It might not be the same one," I grumble. "I've got lots of sticks in my hair." But since I'm not sleepy, I think it must be all right.

I sit down across from her at the tree-stump table. "Fairies don't steal children. That's just something peoples made up."

But as soon as I say this, another memory comes to my mind. The Good Queen is holding a baby, bald and red, showing him to me. I wonder if she did steal a baby-people once. I wonder what happened to it.

I clap my hands to my head. "My brain is having too many thoughts today!" I shout.

Rose nods wisely, as if she knows exactly what I mean. It makes me feel a little better. She pokes at the wax on the top of my jam until it breaks, then takes a scoop with two fingers. I take some, too.

"Oh, Rose," I say, sucking my finger. "I'm in such trouble. That man-people is still there, and now . . ." The thought of his terrible powder makes the jam taste bitter in my mouth. "I can't even say it out loud. It's too awful."

"Don't worry," Rose says. "Soon we will be in the Summer Country."

I'd forgetten about my promise to talk to the Good Queen about Rose. It doesn't seem like such a good idea now.

"Maybe you shouldn't come. Fairies aren't always so nice to peoples."

"You're nice."

"I am foul and horrible!" I insist.

She laughs and comes over to hug me, but I squeal and roll away into the grass. "Please get rid of those daisies. I can't fall asleep now. There's too much to do!"

Rose looks at her necklace and frowns. "Mummy made me promise not to take it off." She looks up at me with an idea in her eyes. "But you could. With the stick."

I reach for the stick behind my ear, but then I remember the singer with the fiery red hair and how miserable the fairies made him. "Maybe your mummy's right. It's keeping you safe."

"But the fairies won't like me if I wear it. They won't let me come with them."

I think of Rose's mother and her bread song. "Rose," I say gently. "You should stay here."

Her eyes grow shiny, and the look on her face is so sad that I almost change my mind. "You said!"

"Can we talk about it tomorrow? Right now I need your help . . ."

"No! The fairies are coming tonight."

For a moment I can only stare. "What . . . did you say?"

"Tonight is when the fairies come to dance. Tonight is Midsummer's Eve."

This must be why my offerings are so good today, why all the houses have horseshoes or bunches of daisies on their doors.

"It can't be." The queen will find that man-people living in the forest. She will be angry. She will bring lightning down from the sky.

"Take off my necklace," Rose begs, so excited she bounces up and down.

"Not now!"

My mind is racing. There is no time. I can't wait until night to play my tricks. I have to play them now, during the day, before the sun sets and the fairies come.

"Rose, can you give me some magic? The man-people has a potion . . ."

"I won't give you anything!" she shouts. "You're a mean fairy!"

"Rose!"

She leaps up and runs to the door.

"Rose, come back!"

10

I HAVE NO CHOICE. EVEN THOUGH it's still daylight, even though I have no magic against the evil powder, I must go to the cottage. The fairies are coming tonight, and I must get rid of the man-people.

The cottage has turned white, and there is a funny smell in the air. The man-people has been painting. I can see his bucket by the barn. The carvings around the door are blue and red.

I recognize this place, I think. *I've seen it before.* If someone were telling me a story about a cottage in the woods, this is the cottage I would picture.

Is this a story? I wonder. *Am I in it?*

I notice something else—a curl of smoke rising from the chimney. The man-people must have figured out about the moss. He must know now that I didn't really put a spell on his hearth.

I edge around the side of the house. The thorny sticks have all been pulled out of the garden and added to the pile of weeds. The man-people must know I didn't curse his garden.

I peer down the well. There is nothing in it but water. He must know I didn't turn his well water into skunk spit and frog pee.

He must know everything. He's seen through all my tricks.

I swallow hard. He is too clever for me.

I had such a good idea of the trick I was going to play next. I told the man-people I would give his cow wings and she would fly to the moon, and so I thought I would lead his cow away and hide her somewhere. After all, she might be on the moon for all he knew. Now my idea doesn't seem so good. My tricks aren't tricky enough, but I don't know what else to do.

My eyes sting. My only hope is that maybe the man-people thinks I am coming tonight, so he hasn't sprinkled his evil powder yet. I don't want to become invisible. I don't want to call and call and have no one hear me. It reminds me of a game Flit and Fleet and the other fairies like to play.

One of them will point at me and say, "I don't see any fairies over there. Do you see a fairy?"

Another will answer: "Well, I see you and I see me, but there's nobody over there."

"It's me!" I say. "I'm right here!"

"Do you hear a fairy?"

"I do not. I hear no fairies."

"I'm here, I'm here, I'm here," I say.

It is a mean game.

I take little steps toward the barn, all the time looking back and forth for the man-people. He must be in the house.

There is no ring of salt now; there are no nails or bits of iron in the grass. For some reason, this upsets me more than anything else. It's as if he thinks he has already won his fight against me.

Slowly, I open the creaky door of the barn, hoping the man-people is not listening.

I've never been *inside* a place before. I've never felt walls all around, squashing me. Is it like being inside the belly of a wolf?

I creep in and shut the door. It's not so bad. Light comes in from some holes in the ceiling and from the spaces between the boards of the walls. The cow takes no notice of me. Suddenly, I'm afraid I may have stepped into the man-people's powder without realizing it.

"Can you see me, cow?" I ask. "Can you hear me?"

She is a beautiful brown cow with big black eyes. I pet her gently on the forehead, and my hand does not go through. No, I don't think I'm a ghost yet.

There is a rope around her neck attached to a ring on the wall. It's a metal ring, but I carefully pick the knot without touching it.

"You're going to be free," I whisper.

"Mooo!" she says.

I take the rope in my hands and pull, but she doesn't come.

"Don't you want to get away from the horrible man-people?" I ask.

"Moo!" she says again, loudly.

"Shhh!" I tell her. "He'll hear."

I can see why she doesn't want to leave. The little barn is snug and small and has a wonderful smell of hay. I'm sure it's as cozy as my nest. I pull the rope again, and she kicks the wall, making the barn shake.

"Oh, don't make so much noise!" I beg. "I'm trying to rescue you."

"MOOOOO!"

"Wicked Nix!" says an angry voice from outside. "Fairy Nix. I know you're in there."

I freeze. There are no windows, and the man-people is at the door. This is why I don't like inside places. You can't get out again.

"There is no one in here," I say.

I don't move, hoping he'll go away again.

"If there is no one there, who is speaking?" the man-people asks.

"Only the cow," I say.

"You don't sound like my cow."

"Only the mouse who lives in the wall."

"Hmmm." I hear the barn door open with a creak.

Quick as a mink, I hide myself in a big pile of hay.

"Nix, foulest of the fairies," the man-people says. "I warned you."

I try to make myself small. I wish I really were a mouse and could scurry away under his feet.

Through the hay I can see him creep-
ing toward me. He has a handful of something. It must be his evil powder, but it's
not in a bottle or a jar; he's just holding
it against his bare skin. It probably only
works on fairies.

"Don't come any closer," I tell him, my
voice shaking. "I might not have any magic,
but I do have my face and when you see it,
you will scream and run away and your hair
will turn white as bone forever . . ."

"I don't have any hair," the man-people says.

I hadn't thought of that. "Well, maybe
your eyes will fall out, then; I'm not sure.
But the queen said I must never show my
face to any peoples. It is too foul for them
to bear."

The man-people hesitates. I can see
that he believes me. "I have this magic

powder." His voice is shaking a little, too. "I'll . . . I'll use it."

I make my decision. It's Midsummer's Eve, and there's no more time. Slowly, I stand up, letting the hay that was covering me fall to the floor.

"Gaze on me in terror, man-people!" I say. "For I am Wicked Nix, the foulest of the fairies!"

The man-people's eyes open wide. "But . . ." he says. "You're not a fairy. You're a boy."

11

I KNOW THAT THE MAN-PEOPLE IS lying to me. I know that I should laugh at him, yell at him, do something. But as soon as the awful words fall out of his mouth, it's like I've been thrown into the icy cold river. I cannot move. I cannot speak.

Boy. He called me a boy.

He takes a step toward me, and I jump back.

"Don't be afraid," he says.

"I'm not!"

But I am. He still has the magic powder clutched in one hand.

"I thought you were something terrible," he says, "but you are only a poor boy lost in the woods. Aren't you?"

That word again. *Boy.* I do not like it. I do not like the softness that's come into his voice. The gentleness. It's the voice I use when I see a deer in the forest and don't want her to run away.

"Do not insult me!" I shout. "I know that a boy is a kind of people—and I am not a people. I am Nix, foulest of the . . ." My voice trails off.

The man-people's face has gone soft and gentle, too. He looks at my bent arm as if he is sorry for me—when he should be afraid. I wish he weren't in front of the door, but he is there, and I am trapped.

"Child, you are not a fairy," he says. "You are a skinny boy with sticks in his hair and dirt on his face. Come and have something to eat in my cottage."

Maybe there is some terrible magic in his words, because when I look at my ragged clothes, my dirty arms, and my thin legs, for a moment I think he might be telling the truth. Am I a boy?

"Stop tricking me with your wicked words—or I will send the bees to sting you and the birds to peck your eyes. I will make stones fly in circles around your head until . . . until you are very dizzy!"

The man-people is quiet for a moment. "I would like to see those magics."

Oh, he's a crafty one.

"And you will," I say. "But now . . . I must go."

I try to push past, but the man-people grabs me. White powder sprays from his hands. I scream. The cow moos.

"It's on me!" I cry, flailing and falling to the ground. "The powder!"

Desperately, I try to brush myself off, but I am covered in gritty flakes. They're on my face, in my hair, up my nose. "No! No!" I cry. "I don't want to disappear! I don't want to be a ghost!"

"I see you," the man-people says, kneeling before me. "It's all right. I still see you, boy. You're not a ghost." He puts his hand on mine. It does not go through. "It's only sawdust. From my carvings. It's not magic."

It takes a minute for his words to sink in. "Sawdust?" I touch some of the powder that fell on the floor and squint at my finger. Then I look at my arms, my body. "I'm not invisible?"

The man-people smiles. "No. I was only trying to trick you. I don't have any more magic than you do."

A trick. Only a trick.

"You're a liar," I say. "Everything you say is a lie." I stand up.

"Wait," he says, but I am already through the barn door, running. "Stop!"

I fly through the forest, leaping over bushes and roots, rushing away from his strange lies.

It was Mr. Green who taught me to howl. I used to be afraid of the wolves at night, even high in my nest, wrapped in my stolen blankets. In winter, their howling was like a song of loneliness and hunger. It got inside my bones, like the cold.

One night, the wolves were very close. The loneliness of their howling became my loneliness. Midsummer's Eve seemed so far away, and I thought I'd never see my fairy family again.

Then I heard Mr. Green's voice in the sighing of the wind, in the clicking of the frozen branches. He reminded me that my family was all around me: The animals sleeping in their dens. The frogs sleeping in the mud under the frozen river. Grandfather Mountain and Grandmother Moon. Even the wolves were my wild brothers, he told me. He said that I should do as they did and howl my loneliness away. And so I did.

Since then I've learned to howl about whatever I feel—fear, anger, happiness, sadness.

I howl now from high in the old oak tree. I howl until the man-people's lie stops crawling around inside my head. I howl until I know who I am again. Nix. Wicked Nix. Foulest of the fairies.

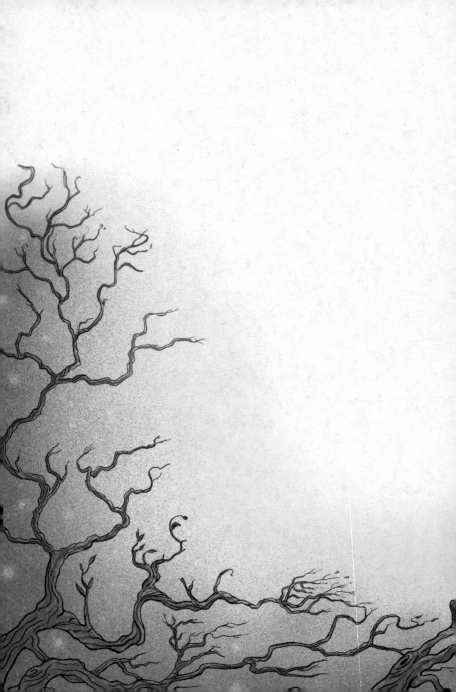

12

I HAVE AN IDEA. ONE LAST IDEA. I
could not trick the man-people. I could
not scare the man-people. But tonight is
Midsummer's Eve, and my time is up. I
bring my basket to his cottage and knock
softly on the door.

"Hello? Anyone in there?"

It is hard not to run away when the door to the cottage opens. I have to keep reminding my feet to stay where they are.

"None of your tricks," I say, looking up at the man-people. "Don't call me a boy or try any of your magic."

He nods slowly.

I hold out my basket. "I've come to trade. These are my very precious things. I might give you some, if you will go away." I do not tell him that I will give him all my things if I have to. Maybe he won't take the one thing I really want to keep.

The man-people eyes the basket suspiciously. "Come inside, and I'll look at what you have."

I take a step back. I'm not going in there.

"All right," he says. "I'll come out."

He comes out and shuts the door, then sits down on the stone path. I sit down, too, with the basket between us.

"This stone I found by the river," I say, pulling out my first treasure. "It's precious because it's so white and smooth, and because it has a face on it." Now that I see it again, it reminds me a little bit of the man-people's bald head. I don't say that, though.

He touches the smooth stone and nods with approval. "What else?"

I set the stone carefully on the ground and pull out the carved animal I took from his window. "This is a fat otter with big teeth."

"That's mine!" he says. "And it's a walrus." He takes it from my hand.

"It's not stealing if you're a fairy," I inform him, but he puts it beside him as if it's his. I pretend I don't care. "There's no such thing as a walrus, anyway."

I take out the next treasure, which is fragile and wrapped in dried grass. "This is a robin redbelly egg that will never become a chick." Gently, I hold it out, blue as sky. "It's precious because it's beautiful, but also because it makes you think about the dead bird inside."

He nods, and I'm glad to see that his face is sad and serious, just as a face should be when talking about dead birds. I set the egg down next to the stone. He points to the basket.

"And?"

"These are the skins of two nighty-night bugs," I say, taking my second-to-last treasures out of the basket.

He wrinkles his nose. "And?"

I don't think he understands. "They walk out of their skins!" I say. "And leave this behind. See"—I hold them out—"the skins even have eyes."

"What else do you have?"

"Gah!" I say in frustration, and I set down the treasure. "I also have good ropes and blankets I could give you. I make my nest with them."

"I think there's something else in that basket."

How does he know?

"Wait! There's this, too." I search my hair for sticks, pulling out three and laying them on the ground. "One of these is definitely magic."

The man-people points at the basket without saying anything, but I don't want to show him my star.

"All these things—the stone, the egg, the fat otter with big teeth, the skins, the magic stick, and my ropes and blankets—I will give you if you leave the forest and never come back."

The man-people hasn't stopped pointing.

"I will also give you a basket to carry them in."

The man-people says nothing. He narrows his eyes and wobbles his pointing finger. Reluctantly, I pull out the last treasure.

"Oh!" the man-people cries.

"It's a real star," I tell him. "From the sky."

He takes it carefully, cupping it in two hands as if it is as fragile as the egg. I see that even though he is an evil man-people, he knows when he is looking at something wonderful. It makes me almost like him.

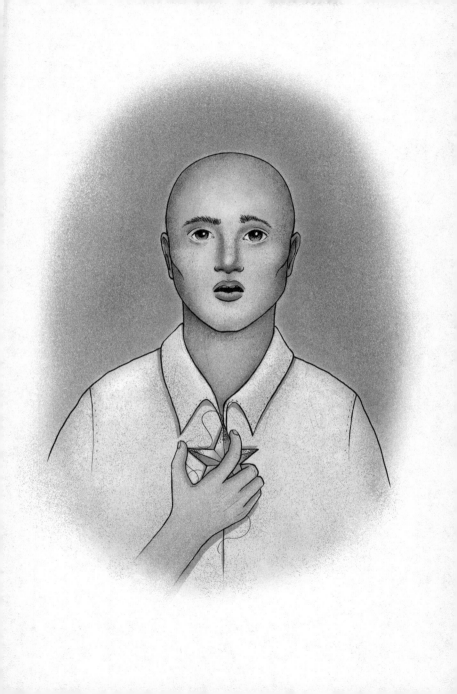

"Where did you get this?"

"The queen pulled it down from the sky for me a long time ago."

The man-people winces as if my words hurt. He stares into my eyes as if he's never seen me before. I stare back.

"All right." He says it so quietly that at first I don't hear him. "All right," he says again. "I'll leave today, if that's what you want." I can hardly believe my ears.

He stands up, holding the star to his chest and looking down at me.

I nod and carefully put my other treasures back in the basket. *He's taking my star*, I think, but that's not so bad. I have my memory. Once I leaned up against the Good Queen's thigh, and her dress was soft as new moss. I remember that. Once she had flour on her apron. I remember that. Once she pulled a star from the sky for me. I don't need to have the star to remember it.

"But first I want you to hear a story," the man-people says.

I glare at him. Hasn't he got enough? I look to the sky, but there's still some time until night, when the fairies will come.

"What kind of story?"

13

"COME IN," HE SAYS, HOLDING OPEN the door.

I don't move. I went into the barn, but this place has even more of an *inside* feeling to it; the floor is made of wood instead of good dirt, and I don't think there are any holes in the ceiling for light to come through. I imagine being squashed and surrounded by walls like the dead bird inside the egg.

"Tell your story out here."

He shrugs. "Stay by the door if you want. I'm going to have some bread and milk."

He goes through the door, but I stay where I am, peering in. Everything is carved and twisty—even things that could be straight, like chairs and table legs. Little animals made of wood are everywhere—on the table, in the corners, above the fireplace. I see rabbits and ducks and birds and deer. I want to go in and pick up each one, but I don't.

The man-people cuts two thick slices from a loaf of bread, then drips honey on them from a pot that looks like a bear. He comes back to the door and hands one to me.

"A man and woman lived here once. Their names were William and Hagar."

He faces one of the twisty chairs to me and sits down. I lean against the doorway and lick the honey from my bread.

"They were wood-carvers, as you can see. They made this place. Oh, the villagers warned them that this is a fairy forest, but they thought they knew all the tricks to keep themselves safe. They hung daisies on their door. They scattered iron in the grass and hung horseshoes on the windows. On Midsummer's Eve, they made a ring of salt all around. After a few years of never seeing a fairy, they thought they had nothing to worry about. They even began to think that maybe fairies were just a story."

The man-people pours two cups of milk, but he does not bring one to me. He just leaves it on the table in the place closest to the door. I have finished my bread, and milk would be the perfect thing to wash it down.

"Then they had a child." He looks at me. "A boy named Nicolas."

He drinks his cup of milk and makes an *mmm* sound as if it is the best milk he's ever tasted.

"Nicolas loved the forest," the man-people goes on. "He was always wandering off. Even though they didn't believe in fairies, William and Hagar kept him safe with daisy chains and were sure to keep him inside on Midsummer's Eve."

The man-people cuts another piece of bread and drips some honey onto it. "Have some more if you like." He puts the bread on the table next to the milk.

I want that piece of bread and honey. I want that milk.

"They had another child. Another little boy."

I put one toe through the door. Nothing terrible happens. After all, it's not a ring of salt. I creep forward. The floor is very flat against my bare feet. The creaking sound it makes is exactly the sound of a tree creaking in the wind.

The man-people looks at me, and I feel trapped by his eyes, but I don't run away. "Nicolas was good to his baby brother, or so I've heard."

"What was his name?" I ask. "The new one?"

"Jonathan," the man-people says. "Nicolas and Jonathan."

I feel as if I have heard those names somewhere before.

"One Midsummer's Eve, little Jonathan caught a cold. His parents were very worried. They didn't watch the older boy the way they should have. They didn't make him a daisy chain to keep the fairies away. For years after, they regretted that."

I edge closer to the table. It's strange to have a ceiling above my head. It feels like it's pressing down on me, so I keep my eyes to the floor and don't look up at it. I reach the bread and push it all into my mouth, taking the cup back to the door.

"Nicolas was stolen away that Midsummer's Eve. By the time Hagar and William got to the meadow, the fairies had already gone back to the Summer Country, taking their son with them."

This must have happened a long time ago, I think, because I've never seen a boy in the Summer Country.

"The queen would have gotten tired of him after a while," I say with my mouth full, thinking of the singer with the fiery red hair.

"So William and Hagar thought," the man-people says, "but it never happened. Every Midsummer's Eve, they would try to find the fairy meadow to beg for their child."

"*Try* to find?" I say. "But it's easy. I've been there lots of times."

The man-people shakes his head. He cuts more bread for me, leaving it on the table. I come and get it, dripping my own honey onto it from the bear pot.

"You see, every Midsummer's Eve, the fairies would play tricks on William and Hagar. Sometimes mysterious lights would lead them from the path. Sometimes they'd hear Nicolas crying, and they'd chase the sound all night, getting more and more lost. Music from the fairy

meadow seemed to come from one direction, then another."

I nod. We fairies do love tricks.

"Once, the fairy queen even made
a life-size doll out of leaves and twigs,
held together with magic. She left it in
front of the cottage on Midsummer's
Eve. William and Hagar were sure it
was their Nicolas come back to them—
until dawn came, and the doll fell apart
in their arms."

The honey is too sweet in my mouth
all of a sudden, and the bread is hard to
swallow. "No," I say. "No. I don't believe
that. The Good Queen is not so cruel."

The man-people only looks at me
with sad eyes. I imagine my fairy friends
laughing at the prank and calling William
and Hagar "stupid peoples."

"Maybe some of the other fairies," I say, "but not the queen."

"All their lives William and Hagar waited for Nicolas," the man-people says. "They always had hope. They even thought he might still be a child when he came back. Time is a strange thing in the Summer Country."

That's true, I think. The singer with the fiery red hair only a spent a few years in the Summer Country, but when he came home, the girl he had left behind was a white-haired old woman, and everyone else he knew was dead and gone.

"Did William and Hagar die?" I ask quietly.

The man-people nods. "And their other son, Jonathan, grew up and went away to become a sailor." He runs a hand over his head. "And he got older. And lost his hair.

And then came back." He smiles, waiting for me to understand.

"Oh," I say. "Is that you? Are you Jonathan?"

"I am," he says. "And Nix, I think you are my older brother, Nicolas."

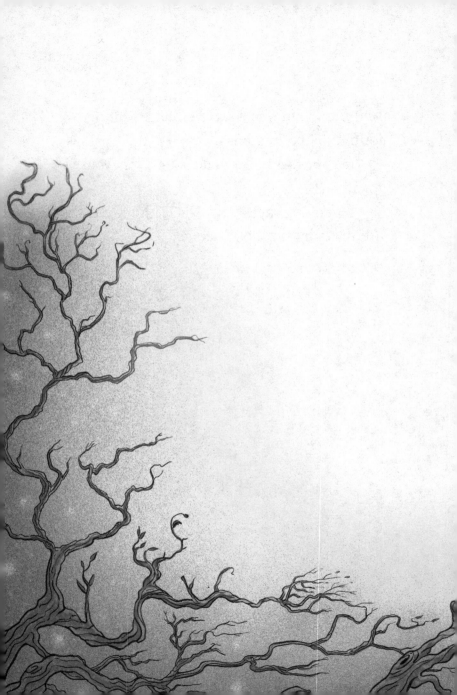

14

"I TOLD YOU NOT TO PLAY TRICKS,"
I say. My stomach feels quivery. Maybe I
ate too fast.

There is a candle on the table. Jonathan
lights it and holds it up. "Look, Nix. Look
at the ceiling."

I look up. Hanging from strings are
carved stars. They are painted silver,

with bits of mirror in their points to make them shine.

I catch my breath. Jonathan is tall enough to touch one and make it spin. Then another.

"Stop it!" I tell him.

He picks up my star from the table and holds it out. It looks exactly the same as the others. "Our parents made them. They told me they carved one for every happy memory in this cottage."

"The queen gave that to me!" I say. "The Good Queen of the Fairies."

"I think it is our mother you are remembering," he says. "Hagar."

"No!" I look to the open door. It's dusk. The fairies will be coming. They might be here already. "It was her. It was the fairy queen."

"Don't go," Jonathan says. "She'll steal

you away again. She'll take you to the Summer Country."

"That's what I want!" I shout. "It's all I've ever wanted!" I turn to leave.

"Wait!" The look on Jonathan's face makes something twist inside me. Above him, stars swing back and forth.

"If you go, then I'm coming with you," he says.

"We missed you, Nix! We missed you, Nix!" the fairies call as I run down the road toward the meadow.

I recognize their voices. There's Fleet and Flit and Wing, and Naughty and Scruff and Dart.

"Where are you?" I shout.

I hear a whirring sound, and I'm sure I see Flit just through the trees, her yellow wings a blur.

Jonathan catches up to me and puts a hand on my shoulder, but I shrug him away. I set off into the forest toward my friends.

"Don't leave the road, Nix," Jonathan warns, but I don't listen.

"I missed you, too!" I yell to the fairies. "The winter was so cold."

They begin to sing a song I know well.

Golden fruit and silver tree,
Flowers sweet and buzzing bee.
Forget your cares and follow me
To the Summer Country.

Endless hills of emerald green,
Beauty as you've never seen,
Ruled over by our midnight queen
In the Summer Country.

Home, I think. They are singing about my home. Lately I have been remembering all the bad things about the fairies—the way they tease me, the way they laughed at the singer with the fiery red hair. But now I remember all the good things—how strange and beautiful they are, like flowers or bats or hummingbirds; how they are always laughing or singing; how they are always thinking of the next trick they are going to play.

I follow their voices, and soon I can see lights flickering in the distance. It must be the fairy bonfires. I must be almost at the meadow.

"Nix, stop!" says Jonathan, who is far behind.

I stop, but not because he told me to. "That's strange," I say. I lift my nose to the air. All around me the fairies are still singing.

"What is it?" Jonathan asks, panting.

"Do you smell something?"

Jonathan sniffs, too. "Is it . . . skunk spit and frog pee?"

"Stinkflowers!" I say. "We're not near the meadow. We're near the pond. This is the wrong way!"

The fairy music fades to nothing, and the forest is quiet again.

"They're tricking us," says Jonathan. "The way they tricked William and Hagar."

"But that's not fair. They're treating us like peoples!"

"Nix," Jonathan says. "We are peoples."

I hear a laugh just off in the trees. Then another.

"I know that's you, Wing!" I call.

The laughing grows louder.

"Watch out, watch out!" the fairy voices say. "The wolves are coming."

Wolves. That can't be right. They're far away on Grandfather Mountain. Then I hear it. A low growl.

There is a rustling in the trees, and a wolf bursts out, his teeth very white.

"Run!" Jonathan says.

We run. Branches whip my legs. Dark has come on quickly, and I can't see very well. Behind us the wolf is snarling. He must be very hungry.

"This way!" I shout.

We splash through the cold river. When we are across, I turn to look at the wolf on the other side.

"Hoooooooooowl!" he says.

All around him, other wolves answer. "Hooooowl! Hooooowl!"

Now there are three wolves, and together they dive into the river after us.

"Come on!" Jonathan says, taking my hand.

We clamber up the slippery riverbank and keep running through the trees. There is no path, only forest. I trip on a tree root and fall flat. I can't get up. I can't run anymore. I'm too tired. Three pairs of yellow eyes race toward us in the dark.

"Keep going!" I yell to Jonathan.

But he throws his body on top of me, just as the wolves leap.

15

THE WOLVES DISAPPEAR AS IF THEY
are made of mist.

"Another trick," Jonathan says.

"Why did you do that?" I snap, getting
up. "Why didn't you run away when I said?"

"Because you are my family."

I stare at Jonathan in the dim light.
"No. Fairies are my family." I hear a giggle

from the trees and turn around. "Fleet! Why are you being so cruel?"

"We can't help it," says a voice.

"The queen says you cannot come to the meadow," says another.

"And so we must play tricks."

"But why doesn't she want to see me?" I ask, my voice small. The fairies don't answer. "Hello? Are you still there?"

All I hear is the hoot of owls and the *chirp-chirp* of nighty-night bugs. I look around, trying to figure out where we are.

"I think we're lost," Jonathan says.

"No. We're near the bramble patch where I found the thorny sticks to put in your garden—but that's even farther away from the meadow than we were before." I sit down on a log. "Those fairies will never let us get there."

My eyes go watery, and a big sigh comes out. Jonathan sits down next to me. He reaches over to take my hand, but I snatch it away.

"You never wanted me to find the meadow! You want me to be a people—but I'm *not* a people! And I'm not your brother!"

"What I want," he says, "is for you to be happy."

Somehow, his being nice makes me feel even worse. "I'll never be happy now."

He puts his hand over mine, and this time I let him. Even though I am wet and cold and miserable, I'm glad I'm not alone.

"I know!" I say. "Mr. Green can help." I should have thought of him before. I jump off the log. "Mr. Green! Mr. Green!"

"Who are you calling, Nicolas?"

"Mr. Green, of course. He always comes when I need him."

"Who?"

How could somebody live in the forest and not know Mr. Green? I wonder.

"He's the face you see in tree bark, sometimes, and the voice you hear in the leaves. You must have met him! He gives good advice."

I call and call, but Mr. Green doesn't come, even though I look for his face in all the dark branches and on all the moonlit tree trunks. I wonder where he could be.

"Do you think maybe Mr. Green was in your imagination?" Jonathan asks. He sees I don't understand. "That's when something's not real."

"Like a walrus?"

"No. It's when you see and talk to things that aren't there."

"Mr. Green is there."

"Sometimes when your imagination is very good, it's hard to tell. Maybe you have been very lonely and made up Mr. Green in your head to keep you company."

This is a terrible thought. "Why are you taking everything away from me?" I shout. "My star. Mr. Green. My friends. Being a fairy. I hate having a little brother!"

My angry words are like magic. They wake a memory. I have said that before.

No one was paying attention to me. The baby was sick. The baby, the baby, the baby. I left the house when no one was looking, and there they were. Fairies. There were fairies in the forest, their eyes like blue sparks.

"I hate having a little brother," I told them.

"No little brothers where we live," a fairy said.

"Come with us," said another. It was Flit. I remember now. I'd never seen anyone with green skin before, and she let me touch her soft wings.

I followed them. They lured me to the meadow, just as they are keeping me away tonight. I don't think I really believed it before. I'm a people. I was stolen.

"Nix," Jonathan says. "You said that Mr. Green comes when you need him. Maybe he hasn't come because you don't need him now. Maybe he knows we can get to the meadow ourselves."

"But how?" I say. "If we get close, Fleet and Flit and the others will stop us with their tricks."

"We are tricky, too," Jonathan tells me. "And nobody knows the forest as well as you do, not even the fairies. I have an idea."

* * *

I cannot see. I cannot hear.

I am wearing a blindfold made from the torn bottom of Jonathan's shirt. My ears are stuffed with ripped-up leaves.

Jonathan is behind me, a hand on my shoulder. He is wearing a blindfold, too, and his ears are also stuffed with leaves.

I walk slowly, one step in front of the other. From the smell, I know we are going past the thorny bushes with the red don't-eat-me berries. We duck under the low branch. Step over the hollow log.

I pat Jonathan's hand, hoping he is not afraid. He has good ideas, for a people.

The fairies are probably all around us, singing their songs, trying to make me see beautiful things to lure me off the path or terrible things to scare me. I wonder if Mr. Green is all around me, too, whispering kind words, or if he is only my imagination.

We are on the deer path now. It goes up and down, but I know every bump and dip. When we pass the place where the green moss grows, I feel my feet sink into the pillowy earth. When we go by the thin-white-lady trees, I hold out my hand and let my fingertips brush their papery bark.

It takes a long time, but I am patient. We cross the river again. We go along the windy path. Finally, I feel the forest open up. I smell the bonfires. I see the light of the moon through my blindfold. We're at the fairy meadow.

Jonathan and I unstuff our ears and uncover our eyes. Jonathan gasps.

The fairies are here, but they are not singing. They are not dancing.

The fairies are all staring at us.

"Don't be afraid," Jonathan whispers, putting his hand in mine.

"I'm not," I say, squeezing it tight.

Some of the fairies are very beautiful, with long shiny hair and wings like a butterfly's or a bird's. Some are scary, with animal faces or clawed bat's wings or pointy antlers on their heads. Most are people-size, but a few are tiny and flit around like bumble-bugs, and some at the back are tall as small trees, very thin and pale and greenish.

I swallow and start toward the hill at the center of the meadow. The crowd parts as we go by. The fairies are all whispering softly to one another, all but the pale and greenish ones, who have no mouths. These only follow Jonathan and me with wide eyes.

The Good Queen stands at the top of the hill in her cloak of midnight, looking down at us. Her hair is white as snow, but her face is young and beautiful. She holds out her arms.

"Darling Nix," she says. "Welcome home."

The sound of her voice is like music. My whole body wants to run toward her. "Is it true?" I ask. "Did you steal me?"

She smiles and shrugs. "You were such a sweet and funny little thing. I told Fleet and Flit that I wanted you, and they got you for me."

"He had a family!" Jonathan shouts.

Around us, fairies grumble and rumble. They don't like to hear someone shouting at their queen.

"All this time I was a people," I say. "Just an ordinary boy."

She shakes her head. "A special boy. A patient boy who waited all through the winter for Midsummer's Eve to come again. You must love me very much."

"Oh, I do."

She puts her hand to her heart. "And I love you, Nix."

I want to believe her more than any-thing, but a question jumps into my mouth. "Then why did you leave me last Midsummer's Eve? Why was I alone in the forest for a whole year?"

The Good Queen's eyes go to her feet. All around her, the fairies sigh. Her face is even more beautiful when it is sad.

"That was all a mistake. I thought you had run away. I was so unhappy."

Around her, fairies nod and repeat her words. "Unhappy. So unhappy."

"You shouldn't believe her, Nix," Jonathan says. "Why did she try to keep us away from the meadow just now?"

"Yes," I say. "Why did you try to keep us away from the meadow?"

"Oh," says the queen. "Well. The truth is, I was so unhappy that you were gone—"

"So unhappy," repeat the fairies.

"—that I decided to steal another little people to replace you. Don't be jealous, Nix."

The queen pulls back one side of her dark cloak and steps away. There, sitting on the grass, is Rose the Wise.

16

"ROSE," I SAY. "WHY AREN'T YOU wearing your daisy chain?"

Rose doesn't answer. She only sits quietly in the grass, smiling.

"It wasn't easy to get her to take it off," the Good Queen says. "But when Flit told her she could come and live with us, she finally did."

It's my fault. I told Rose all about the Summer Country and how wonderful it is. I made her want to come.

"You'll get tired of her," I say. "The way you got tired of the singer with the fiery red hair." *The way you got tired of me.*

The queen looks lovingly down at Rose. "Surely not."

Maybe Rose would be happy in the Summer Country, I think. She'd laugh and dance and play tricks. She'd have fairies for friends. The Good Queen would pull down stars from the sky just for her.

But then, it wasn't the Good Queen who gave me my star, was it? It was Hagar. My mother.

Rose has a mother, too—a mother who makes bread and puts Rose's hair in bows and makes her sit still for a nice dinner. Rose has a mother who loves her.

"I think," I say, "that Rose should go back home."

There is a rustle of surprise through the fairy crowd.

The queen raises an eyebrow as if I've said something funny, but her voice is icy cold when she speaks: "I take what I want."

I step forward. Jonathan is still holding my hand and comes with me, though I think I feel him shaking with fear. Or maybe that's me.

"No," I say. "Rose has a family."

The queen seems to grow taller. For a moment, I think she will do something terrible—call down a bolt of lightning from the sky—but then she smiles.

"I will make you a bargain," she says. "I will allow you to take Rose home. But in return, you must never tell anyone else how you managed to see through our fairy tricks—and you must promise never to come to the meadow again on Midsummer's Eve."

I'm about to answer, but she raises her hand.

"However, if you choose, you may come with Rose and me to the Summer Country. You will be one of the fairies again, and all will be forgiven."

My heart leaps like a deer. Everything could be like it was. I wouldn't be cold. I wouldn't be hungry. Time would be slow and sweet as honey again, and everything would be like a dream. Jonathan squeezes my hand tight, but he doesn't tell me what to do.

"No," I say. "Rose is special. Rose needs . . . something better."

Jonathan whispers: "And so do you."

"I agree to your bargain," I say. "I won't tell how I saw through your tricks, and I won't come to the meadow on Midsummer's Eve—not ever."

The queen's face is hard as stone, but she gestures to the little girl on the ground. "Take her, then. I always keep my word. Take her and go."

"Come with us, Rose," I say, holding out my hand.

From somewhere in the crowd of fairies, I think I hear a laugh.

Rose has been quiet all this time. Very quiet. In fact, I have never seen her sit still for so long.

With a cry, I remember Jonathan's story about the doll that fooled William and Hagar.

"That's not the real Rose," I say. "That's a fake made of twigs and mud and magic!"

From out behind the queen's black cloak comes a little girl who dances in circles on the grass.

"Ha-ha-ha! Fa-li-la!" she sings. "I told you Nix is clever. He saw through your tricky trick!"

"That's the real Rose," I say.

The false Rose tips over, its eyes open and staring.

"Impossible!" The queen cries. She points a long finger at me. "You are a mere people, and yet you know all my secrets. I cannot allow it."

"Run, Nix!" Jonathan cries.

But suddenly there are fairies all around us, threatening with horns and antlers and pointy teeth. We cannot get away.

The queen raises her arms, and dark clouds rush to the sky above her, blotting out the moon. I know that she is going to call down the lightning.

"We made a bargain!" I shout. "You said you always keep your word!"

Thunder cracks.

"I won! I got to the meadow. I saw through all your tricks!"

Jonathan throws himself between the queen and me.

"Stop doing that!" I say to him. "I'm the older brother!" But it's nice to have someone to hide behind, even though I know it won't do any good.

The queen looks huge now, and lightning sparks around her fingertips. The skies flash. I squeeze my eyes tight shut.

"Enough!" cries a voice, a low, deep voice that seems to shake the ground.

I open my eyes.

All is quiet.

From out of the forest comes a gigantic person who seems to be made of trees. His arms are great branches. His legs are enormous roots. His face is a pattern of swirling leaves.

Mr. Green, the fairies whisper to one another. *Mr. Green is here.*

The tall, pale fairies with no mouths all bow low to the ground before him.

"It's Mr. Green!" I say. Jonathan's eyes are wide. "I must have a very good imagination."

"I may have been wrong about that," my brother says.

"The boy is right, fairy queen," Mr. Green says. "You made a bargain. Do you mean to break it?"

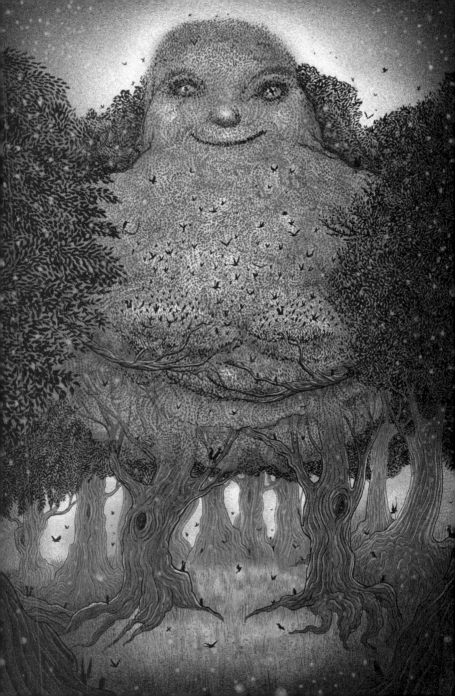

The queen looks smaller. The clouds above her rush away as quickly as they came, and the moon is bright again.

"I . . ." she begins. "But . . ." She stamps her foot. "Why would you side with one of them?"

Mr. Green makes a grumbly sound: *Mmmmmm.*

He comes to the middle of the meadow, his root-legs trailing dirt behind him. When he stops and raises his arms, it is as if we are all suddenly in the forest. I look up and up. I can see the moon through the leaves of his face.

"I am the forest," Mr. Green says to the Good Queen. "And Nicolas is forest born. I protect everything under my branches—the grass and the grouse, the ferns and the fireflies, the bats and the bears." I hear wood creaking and groaning as he bends down to look into the queen's face. "Nicolas is one of my dear little weeds. You would do well to remember that, oh queen who only visits me once a year."

"Yes, Mr. Green," the queen says meekly.

Mr. Green straightens up, and I hear groaning and creaking again. "Now," he says to Jonathan and me. "If I remember the ways of peoples, Rose should be in bed by now. Please take her home."

17

I AM TIRED. SO TIRED. I FALL ASLEEP in the garden when Jonathan is talking to Rose's mother. I fall asleep again on my feet while walking back to the oak tree. When I wake up, I am not in my nest. I am in a little bed.

I'm sure I have been in this bed before, but it was bigger then. I remember the carved flowers on it, pretty as Rose's garden. I remember its softness underneath me. I remember this feeling of being warm and safe.

The room is yellow in the candlelight. Jonathan is at the table carving something out of wood.

"In the morning, I will go back to my nest," I tell him.

Jonathan stops. "All right."

He sounds a little sad. I wonder if he is lonely.

"But I could come back sometimes."

Jonathan picks up his work again. "I'd like that." There are wood curls on the floor, and he nudges them into a pile with his foot. "I could teach you how to carve."

I yawn, pulling the bed covers around me. I could teach Jonathan where the best berries are. And how to catch a snake.

And all the names of things. Without an older brother, there are probably a lot of things he doesn't know.

"Of course . . . you could stay here," he says. "If you wanted."

I'm not sure about that, so I don't answer.

"You are a people, you know."

That's true. I'll probably have to start doing people-y things, like taking baths and eating with a fork. Horrible.

"Jonathan," I say. "Why didn't you ever get married and have children?"

"I just didn't . . . I don't know. It didn't happen."

I sit up. "You could still find some lady," I tell him. "One who doesn't mind no hair."

"Go to sleep. We'll talk in the morning."

I try, but I am wide-awake now. The bed is too close to the ground. The fluffy covers are too comfortable. I kick them off.

The truth is, I want to stay with Jonathan, but I know that if I do, things will change. I'm afraid I'll forget how to howl. I'm afraid I'll forget how to tell one bird from another just by the sound of her wings. I'm afraid that Mr. Green will whisper secrets to me, and I won't hear them because I will be inside a cottage. What if he is whispering to me right now?

I'm about to tell Jonathan that I have to go back to my nest right away, but then I see what he is carving. A star. A five-pointed star.

He told me that our parents carved a star for every happy memory, and I wonder if the happy memory that he is carving is of finding me.

I sigh. I love my nest, but Jonathan can't come there. He might fall out.

"I'll stay," I tell him. "You are my little brother, and you need me to take care of you."

"That's true," Jonathan says. "I do."

Acknowledgments

The idea for *Wicked Nix* came to me years ago in Peter Carver's wonderful Writing for Children class, but I could never get it right. I am very grateful to early readers Georgia Watterson, Hadley Dyer, Paula Wing, and Kathy Stinson for helping me to finally find Nix's voice, and to Susan Van Metre, whose brilliant advice helped me flesh out the book and uncover the heart of the story.

Many thanks go to my agent, Steven Malk; Erica Finkel and Alyssa Nassner at Abrams Books; Suzanne Sutherland at HarperCollins Canada; and the many others who had a hand in this book's publication.

I gratefully acknowledge the support of the Canada Council for the Arts that came in the form of a grant to complete this work.

Finally, thank you to Jaime Zollars for her beautiful illustrations and for making me one of those authors with a map at the beginning of her book, something I've always wanted to be.

LENA COAKLEY is the author of *Witchlanders* and *Worlds of Ink and Shadow*. She concentrated in creative writing at Sarah Lawrence College and now lives in Toronto.

JAIME ZOLLARS is an illustrator of children's books. She is inspired by fairy tales, Flemish painters, and flea-market photographs. She lives in Charleston, South Carolina.